AMIFIKA

AMIFIKA

by Lucille Clifton · illustrated by Thomas DiGrazia

E. P. Dutton   New York

Text copyright © 1977 by Lucille Clifton
Illustrations copyright © 1977 by Thomas DiGrazia

Library of Congress Cataloging in Publication Data

Clifton, Lucille, date   Amifika.

SUMMARY: Fearful that his father won't remember him
after being away in the army, little Amifika
looks for a place to hide.

[1. Fathers and sons—Fiction]
I. DiGrazia, Thomas.   II. Title.
PZ7.C6224Am   [E]   77-5887   ISBN: 0-525-25548-6

Published in the United States by E. P. Dutton, a Division
of Sequoia-Elsevier Publishing Company, Inc., New York
Published simultaneously in Canada by Clarke,
Irwin & Company Limited, Toronto and Vancouver

Editor: Ann Durell   Designer: Meri Shardin
Printed in the U.S.A.   First Edition
10 9 8 7 6 5 4 3 2 1

For Anna Merle
and Scott Venture,
special people

Amifika's Mama had been laughing
and singing all day.

And when Cousin Katy came to visit after he had gone to bed, Amifika could hear them talk.

"Oh Katy, Katy, got a letter from Albert and he be home tomorrow for good!"

"Hallelujah." Cousin Katy sounded like she was laughing too. "Thank God, Jamilla, after this long time!"

"Yes, his army days are done." Amifika could hear the music in his Mama's voice.

"But Jamilla, girl." Cousin Katy was rocking in the chair by the stove. "Where ever will he fit in these two little rooms? You all don't have any space now!"

"Don't worry, Katy." Amifika's Mama sounded sure. "We'll just get rid of something he won't miss. Lot of stuff around here he won't even remember."

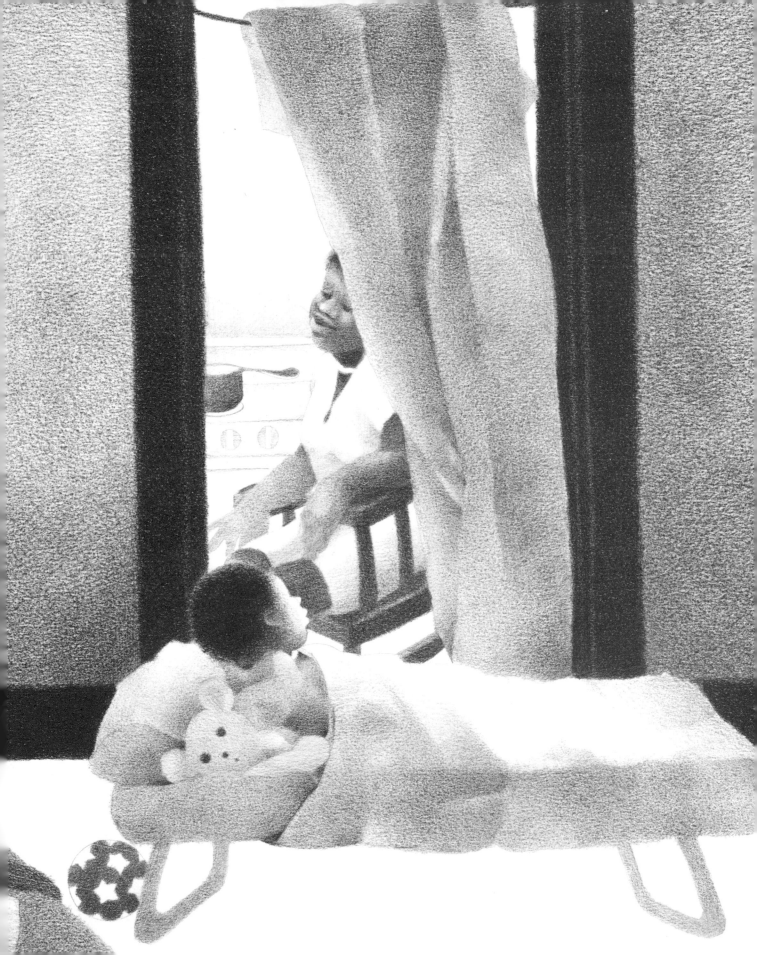

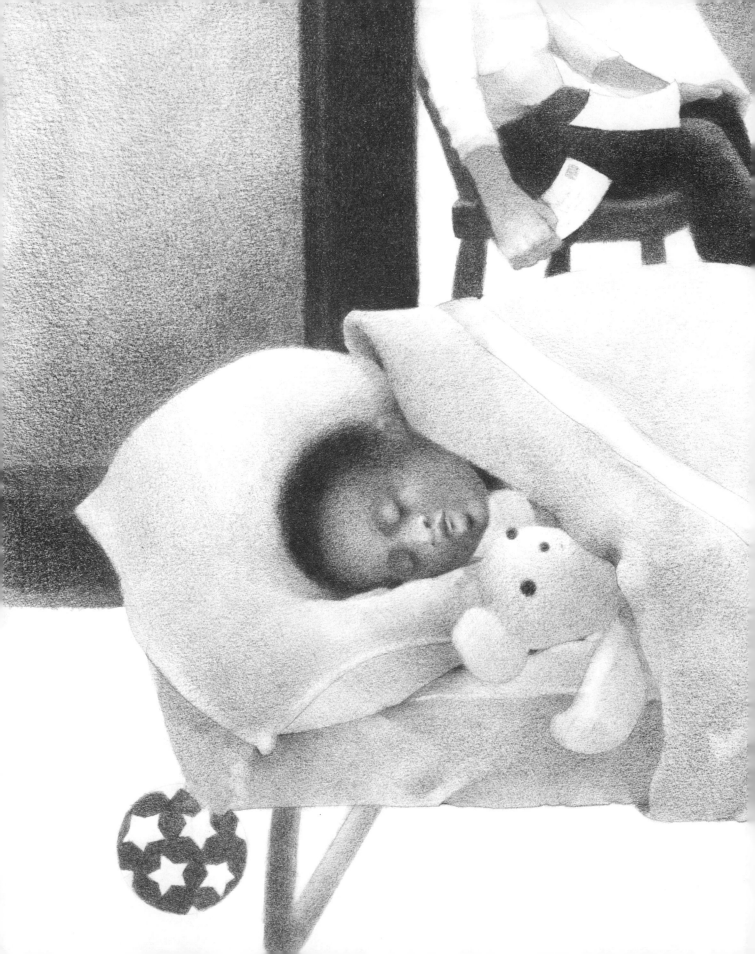

Amifika turned his head and closed his eyes tight and tried to remember his Daddy, but he couldn't. Just something dark and warm that kept moving in his mind.

"If I don't remember him, how he gon' remember me?" he thought. "I be what Mama get rid of. Like she said, he can't miss what he don't remember. I be the thing they get rid of."

After a while, he fell asleep.

Next day Amifika decided to find a place to hide.

"If they get rid of me, they have to find me first," he whispered to himself. There weren't many good hiding places in the two rooms.

He squeezed up under the oilcloth by the bottom of the sink, but it was wet under there and he started sneezing.

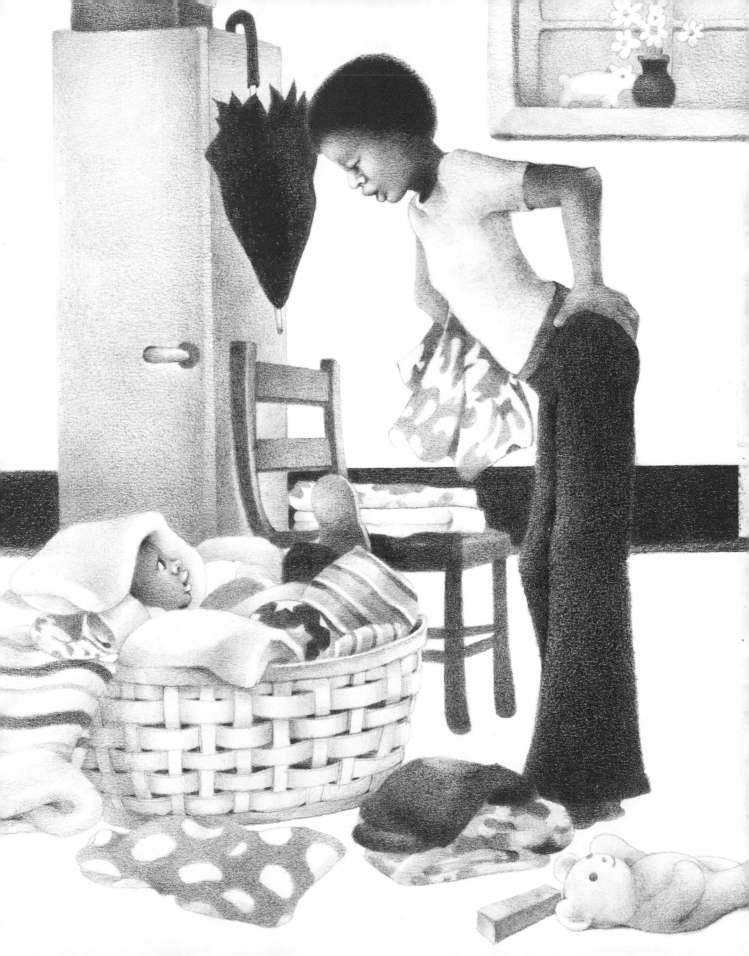

He jumped in the clean clothes basket and piled towels and sheets on top of his head, but when his Mama got ready to fold clothes, she shooed him away.

"What's the matter with you, Amifika? You in my way now."

Don't I know it," Amifika whispered to himself.

He went into Mama's closet and hid among the dresses. Everything smelled sweet and warm and homey, and Amifika thought he could just stay there forever.

"How come we got to change and everything," he mumbled, "just because of some old body I don't even remember nothin' about? How he gon' remember me," he mumbled louder, "if I can't remember him? Shoot, anyhow." He said right out loud, "Shoot!"

"Amifika, boy, what's wrong with you?" His Mama had heard him. "Come out of there and stop that yelling. Go let Katy in."

Amifika went and opened the door. Cousin Katy was
standing there. She was holding a broom and some
big paper bags.

"We'll get rid of something now," she said.

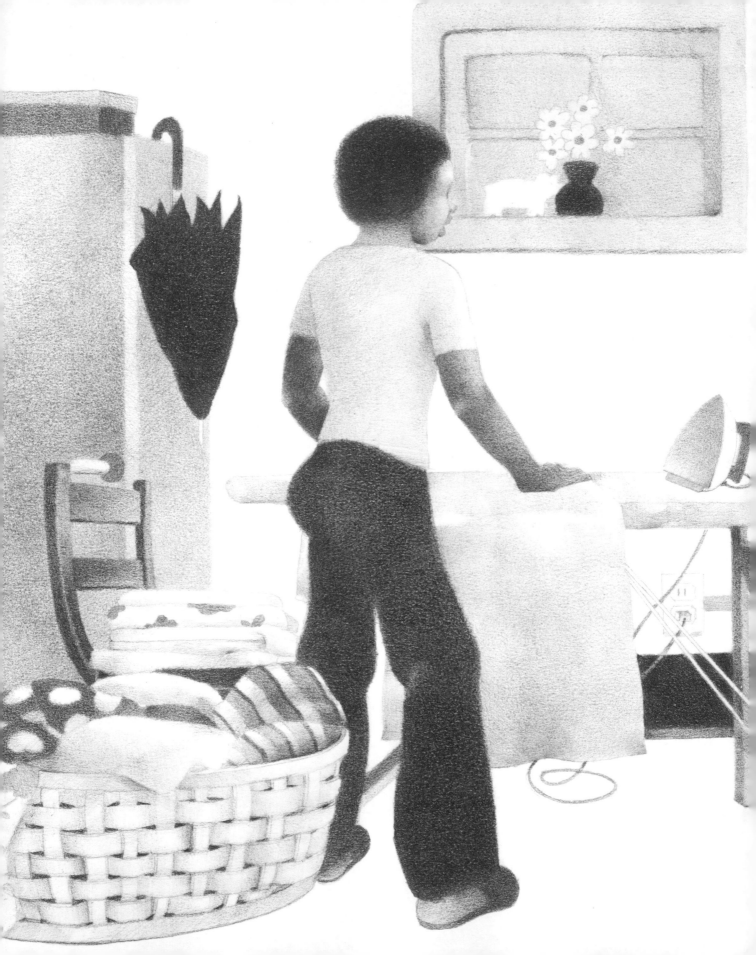

Amifika ran past her and out the door.

"I can't remember!" he shouted. "I just can't!"

Far down the yard between the tree and the fence there was a space just big enough for Amifika. He sat down there on the grass and leaned against the tree and looked at the rooming house where he had lived all his life.

"How could they get rid of me so easy?" he whispered. He felt his eyes getting wet and tired. "I'll just stay here and build me a tree house and take care of myself." He closed his tired eyes.

Everything was dark and turning around and around him and rocking him. He just lay against the tree and let it rock.

"He waking up now." Mama's voice sounded all happy and dancing. Amifika opened his eyes wide. He was in his own room again and a man was holding him and kissing him and shaking his head and halfway laughing and crying.

"Wake up, boy." The man looked in Amifika's face. "Do you remember me?"

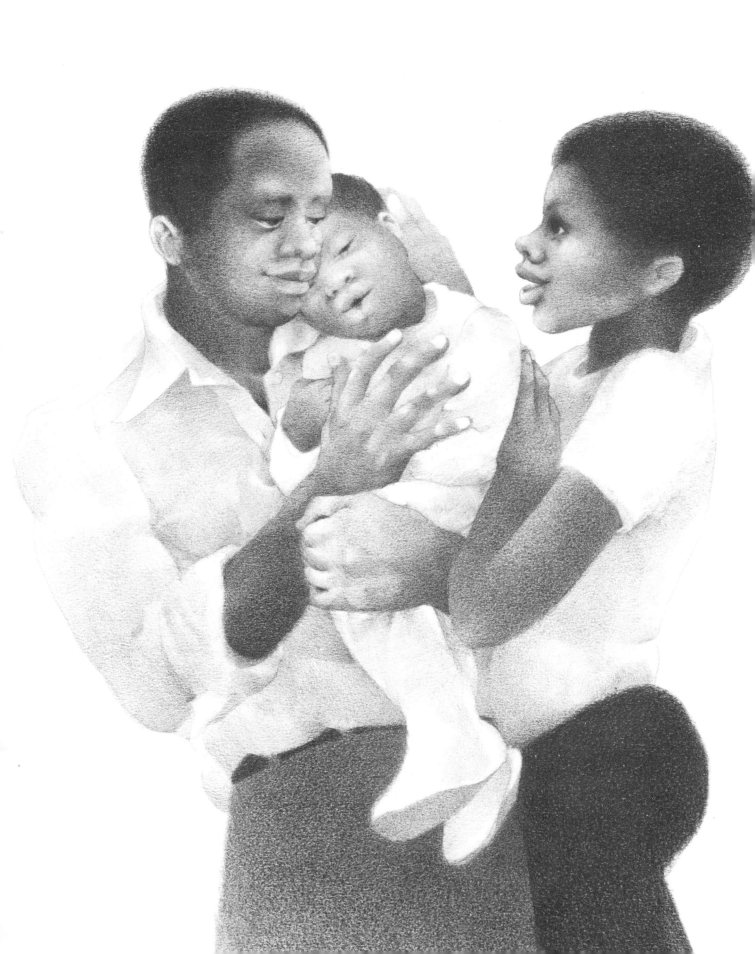

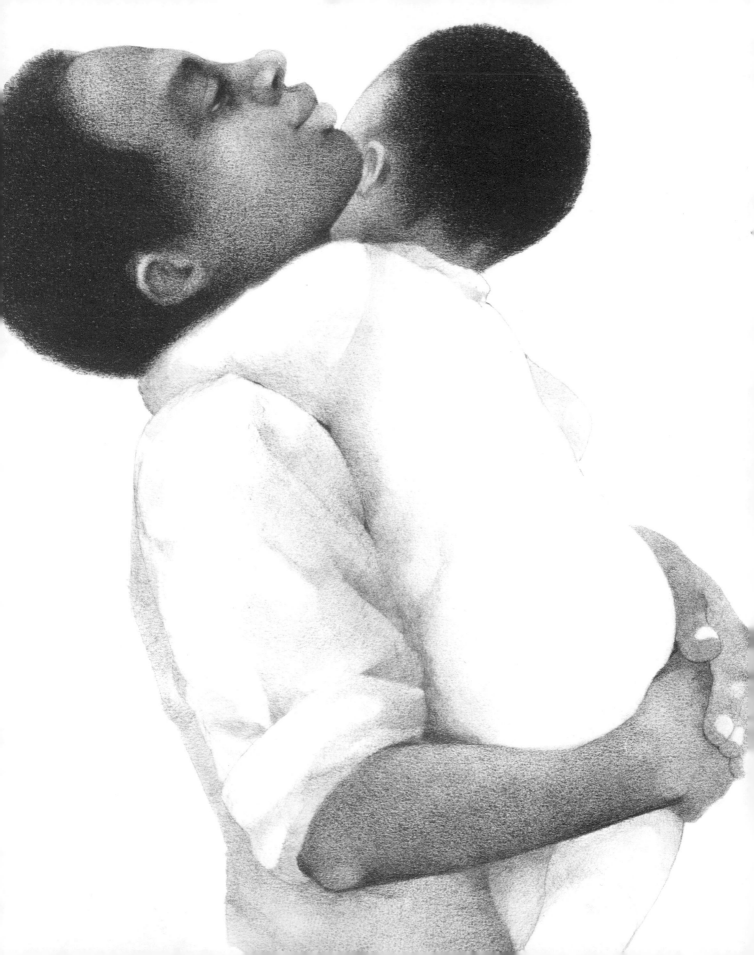

And all of a sudden the dark warm place came together in Amifika's mind and he jumped in the man's arms and squeezed his arms around the man's neck just like his arms remembered something.

"You my own Daddy! My Daddy!" he hollered at the top of his voice and kept hollering as his Daddy held him and danced and danced all around the room.

LUCILLE CLIFTON has written numerous books for children, including *The Boy Who Didn't Believe in Spring, Don't You Remember?* and *Good, Says Jerome.* A mother of six children, she is aware of fears prompted by a child's imagination. In *Amifika,* she portrays them with sensitivity and humor. Mrs. Clifton and her family live in Baltimore, Maryland.

THOMAS DiGRAZIA, a graphic designer and poet, as well as an illustrator, chose to illustrate *Amifika* because he was moved by the story and felt deeply for the boy. He has illustrated many books for children, including *Hold My Hand* by Charlotte Zolotow and *Walk Home Tired, Billy Jenkins* by Ianthe Thomas. Mr. DiGrazia lives in New York City with his wife and two daughters.

The title display type is Typositor Cheltenham Bold Open. The text and other display type is Baskerville, set in foundry and linotype. The art was drawn in pencil, and the book was printed by offset at Halliday Lithographers.